BEST FRIENDS

written by Margaret Cleveland • photographs by Elizabeth Hathon

HARCOURT BRACE & COMPANY

Orlando   Atlanta   Austin   Boston   San Francisco   Chicago   Dallas   New York
Toronto   London

Sometimes happy.

Sometimes sad.

Sometimes sorry.

Sometimes glad.

Sometimes silly.

Sometimes mad.

Always best friends.